MICHAEL GARLAND

Mystery Mansion

a LOOK AGAIN book

Dutton Children's Books • New York

To my brother, John

CIP Data is available.

Published in the United States 2001 by Dutton Children's Books,
a division of Penguin Putnam Books for Young Readers
345 Hudson Street, New York, New York 10014
www.penguinputnam.com
Designed by Benjamin Wright

Printed in Hong Kong
First Edition
ISBN 0-525-46675-4
1 3 5 7 9 10 8 6 4 2

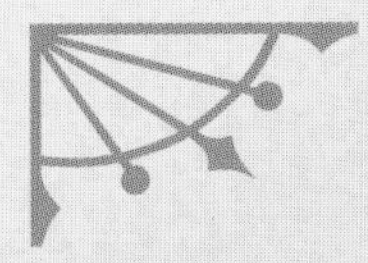

Dear Reader,

This book is a puzzle—
A hide-and-seek game.
On every new page
Is a challenge to tame.

There are letters to watch for
That spell out a clue
About what I've planned
For my nephew and you.

Be looking for frogs
And my wild butterflies,
Some lizards and snakes
And birds with bright eyes.

Mice, bats, and fish
Are everywhere, too,
And three magic creatures
Are waiting for you.

Check the book's covers—
The front and the back.
Most things are well hidden
So try to keep track.

Take a pencil and paper
And carefully look.
Make a list of the things
That you find in this book.

My list's at the end,
Take yours and compare.
If the two don't agree,
There's no need to despair.

Look again at these pages,
And as you go through
You'll see, if you're careful,
My numbers are true.

—Aunt Jeanne

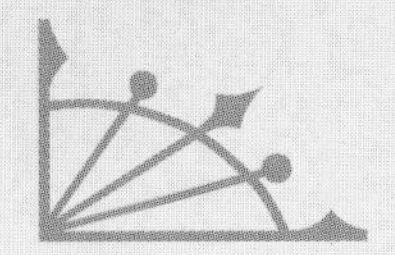

Tommy always liked to check the mail, but today was special. He thought there might be some cards for him among the magazines and bills. A pale yellow envelope caught his eye, so he opened it first.

Dear Tommy,

I've finally returned
From an extended vacation,
With so much to tell
My much-loved relation.

On the trip I collected
My own little zoo.
I chose all the creatures
Especially for you.

Come for a visit,
Yip-yippee, yahoo!
I can't wait to see you,
My favorite nephew.

—Aunt Jeanne

Tommy was so excited when he read his aunt's note that he didn't notice any of the animals around him. But *you* can see them, can't you?

Aunt Jeanne's mansion was only a few blocks away. When he reached the front gates and peered through them, Tommy thought to himself that the house looked different from the last time he had seen it. The sound of something slithering through the grass distracted him, but then he noticed a note stuck to the gate.

Early or late,
It's all the same.
It makes no difference,
I'm glad that you came!

Open the gate,
Come up to the house.
I am the cheese,
You are the mouse.

If Tommy hadn't been in such a hurry to find his aunt, he might have noticed all the bats and birds, butterflies and lizards, snakes and mice, frogs and fish that were right nearby. Keep your eyes open—there are creatures hiding everywhere in this book. How many can you count?

Some people might have been frightened by the odd old house with its creaky towers and dark windows that seemed to watch for the uninvited. But Tommy wasn't the least bit scared—he knew the mansion was just a little different, in the same way his Aunt Jeanne was, well, just a little different. When he reached the giant front door he found another note.

Don't bother knocking,
Just come right in.
Find the next note
And your tour will begin.

Tommy thought it was a little mysterious that Aunt Jeanne was nowhere to be found. After all, he had come to see *her*. And where were the creatures she had mentioned in her first note? Just inside the door, another note dangled from a string.

You don't need me
To lead you around.
Follow my notes
And what's lost will be found.

Explore every corner
Of my happy home.
There's something of interest
Wherever you roam.

One thing to remember
As you wander about:
The kitchen's forbidden,
You have to keep out!

What's so special about the kitchen? Tommy wondered. What could be in there?

Tommy found another note tacked to the entrance of the living room. Aunt Jeanne must have left them everywhere, he thought as he pulled down the note to read it.

I'm happy you're here
On this special day.
Go into the gallery
And don't lose your way.

Tommy gazed at the pictures that covered the walls of the gallery. Then he noticed a beautiful parrot with a note in its beak.

Ponder my pictures—
I think you'll agree,
The more that you look,
The more you will see.

The parlor is next
If you've finished up here.
A challenge awaits you—
There's no need to fear.

Tommy took one last look at the paintings, and then walked into the parlor. In the center of the empty room, he found a strange stack of objects. The note propped up against them said:

The secret, you see,
To winning this game
Is to write the first letter
Of each object's name.

You'll know why you've come
If you juggle this jumble.
Try different spellings;
Take care not to fumble.

When you've finished your task
And the answer is found,
Move along to the greenhouse
And look all around.

FRESH
דג

After he had unscrambled the letters, Tommy felt more excited than ever. He raced down the hall to the greenhouse. There was a net hanging from the doorknob, and inside the net was a note. Tommy read it and then entered the steamy room, which was filled with exotic plants and clouds of butterflies.

They're so hard to catch—
They like to be free.
The trick is to find
The one with the key.

You'll need the key
To unlock the door
That leads to the garden—
There's more to explore.

I

Tommy turned the key in the lock and stepped out into the garden. A path bordered by thick bushes led to a fishpond. On the first bush, Tommy spotted a note stuck to a thorn. He carefully pulled it free. The note puzzled him. He looked all around, but since he didn't see anything out of the ordinary, he kept walking.

It's time to reflect
On this pretty scene.
Look up and then down,
To see what I mean.

mariposa

As Tommy continued to wander around the peculiar garden, he began to feel a little hungry. Was he ever going to find his Aunt Jeanne? Just then he saw another note tucked between the leaves of an oddly shaped hedge.

None but the clever
Can defeat my maze.
This is the entrance
On which you gaze.

Tommy entered the maze and began to follow the winding path. He hadn't gone far when he heard something crinkle under his foot. Half hidden by pebbles was another note.

Round and round's
The way to go.
Find the center
And Cupid's bow.

After many wrong turns, switchbacks, and dead ends, Tommy began to think he would never get to the center of the maze. At last, he came to an opening in the hedges and saw the statue of Cupid. It was pushed aside to reveal the entrance to a tunnel. Tommy climbed up on the pedestal to reach the note on Cupid's arrow.

It's dark in there,
But go down the hole.
Follow the tunnel
As if you're a mole.

Don't be discouraged—
You're almost done.
A little more work—
The surprise will be fun!

The damp, spooky tunnel seemed to go on forever. Something crept across the floor and bats flapped all around. Flickering candlelight was all that helped guide Tommy as he tiptoed along. At the very end of the tunnel, he came upon two small doors. A note was taped to one of them.

Behind these doors
My mysteries hide.
Are you brave enough?
Only you can decide.

Should you open the doors
And come on through?
Or retrace your steps?
It's all up to you.

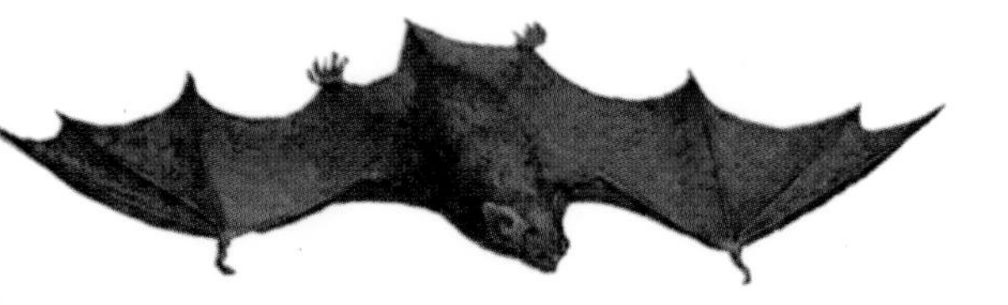

H A P P Y B
Flour
Lézard
Sugar

RTHDAY

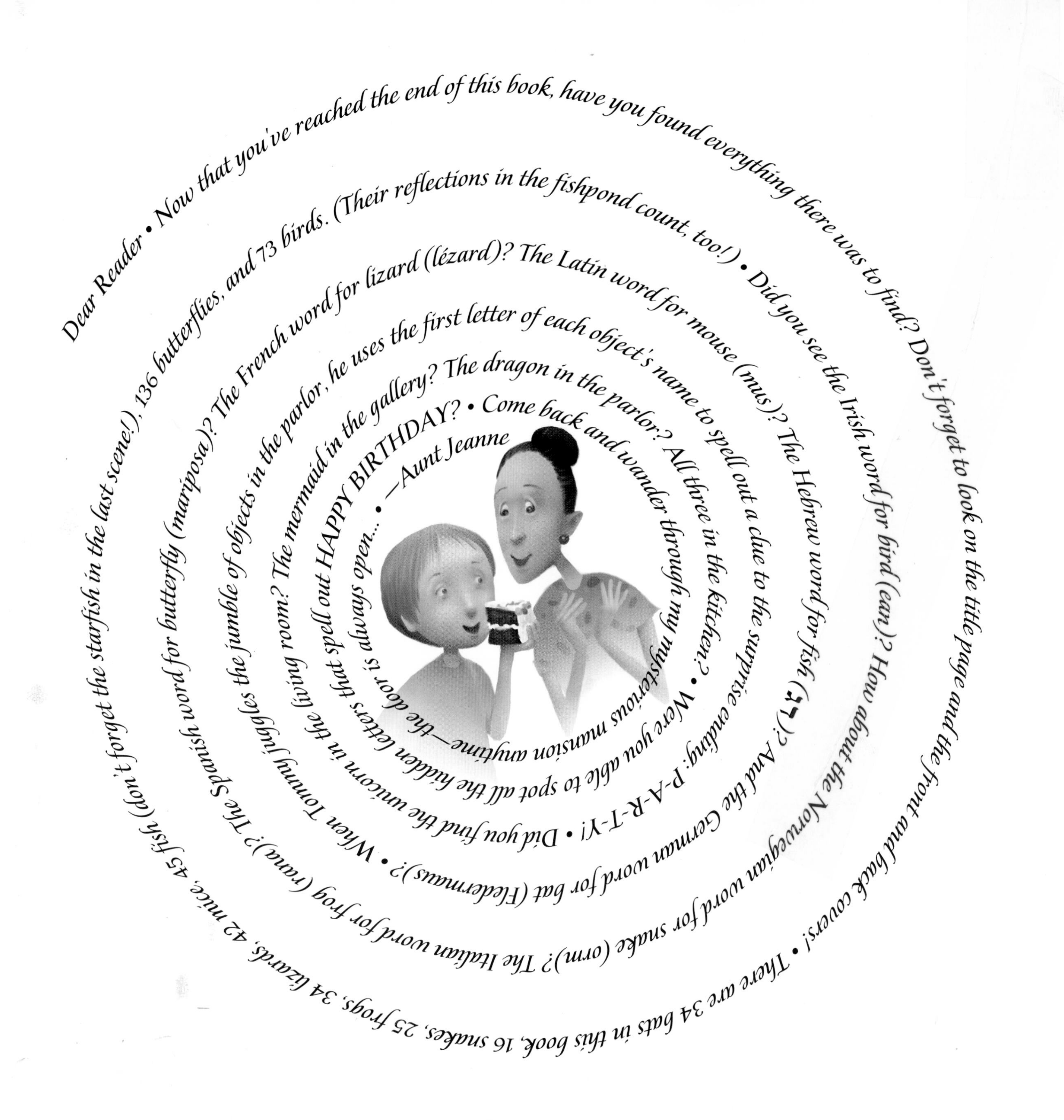

Dear Reader • Now that you've reached the end of this book, have you found everything there was to find? Don't forget to look on the title page and the front and back covers! • There are 34 bats in this book, 16 snakes, 25 frogs, 34 lizards, 42 mice, 45 fish (don't forget the starfish in the last scene!), 136 butterflies, and 73 birds. (Their reflections in the fishpond count, too!) • Did you see the Irish word for bird (éan)? How about the Norwegian word for snake (orm)? The Italian word for frog (rana)? The Spanish word for butterfly (mariposa)? The French word for lizard (lézard)? The Latin word for mouse (mus)? The Hebrew word for fish (דג)? And the German word for bat (Fledermaus)? • When Tommy juggles the jumble of objects in the parlor, he uses the first letter of each object's name to spell out a clue to the surprise ending: P-A-R-T-Y! • Did you find the unicorn in the living room? The mermaid in the gallery? The dragon in the parlor? All three in the kitchen? • Were you able to spot all the hidden letters that spell out HAPPY BIRTHDAY? • Come back and wander through my mysterious mansion anytime—the door is always open... • —Aunt Jeanne